P9-DVO-634

Learning to Read, Step by Step!

Ready to Read   Preschool–Kindergarten
• big type and easy words • rhyme and rhythm • picture clues
For children who know the alphabet and are eager to begin reading.

Reading with Help   Preschool–Grade 1
• basic vocabulary • short sentences • simple stories
For children who recognize familiar words and sound out new words with help.

Reading on Your Own   Grades 1–3
• engaging characters • easy-to-follow plots • popular topics
For children who are ready to read on their own.

Reading Paragraphs   Grades 2–3
• challenging vocabulary • short paragraphs • exciting stories
For newly independent readers who read simple sentences with confidence.

Ready for Chapters   Grades 2–4
• chapters • longer paragraphs • full-color art
For children who want to take the plunge into chapter books but still like colorful pictures.

STEP INTO READING® is designed to give every child a successful reading experience. The grade levels are only guides; children will progress through the steps at their own speed, developing confidence in their reading. The F&P Text Level on the back cover serves as another tool to help you choose the right book for your child.

Remember, a lifetime love of reading starts with a single step!

For Cooper and Chase
Love, Granola

Copyright © 1998, 2015 by Sherry Shahan

All rights reserved. Published in the United States by Random House Children's Books, a division of Random House LLC, a Penguin Random House Company, New York. This work was originally published in a different form as a Random House Pictureback® book by Random House Children's Books, New York, in 1998.

Step into Reading, Random House, and the Random House colophon are registered trademarks of Random House LLC.

Photograph credits: pp. 5, 6, 9 (top), 11, 16, 24–25, 27, 31: courtesy of Ronnie Goyette.

Visit us on the Web!
StepIntoReading.com
randomhouse.com/kids

Educators and librarians, for a variety of teaching tools,
visit us at RHTeachersLibrarians.com

Library of Congress Control Number: 2014940140
ISBN 978-0-385-37189-6 (trade) — ISBN 978-0-375-97189-1 (lib. bdg.) —
ISBN 978-0-375-98178-4 (ebook)

Printed in the United States of America
10 9 8 7 6 5 4 3 2 1

This book has been officially leveled by using the F&P Text Level Gradient™ Leveling System.

STEP INTO READING®

A SCIENCE READER

The Little Butterfly

by Sherry Shahan

Random House New York

The sun shines on wildflowers.
A tiny egg hides under a leaf.

The egg splits open.

A caterpillar crawls out.

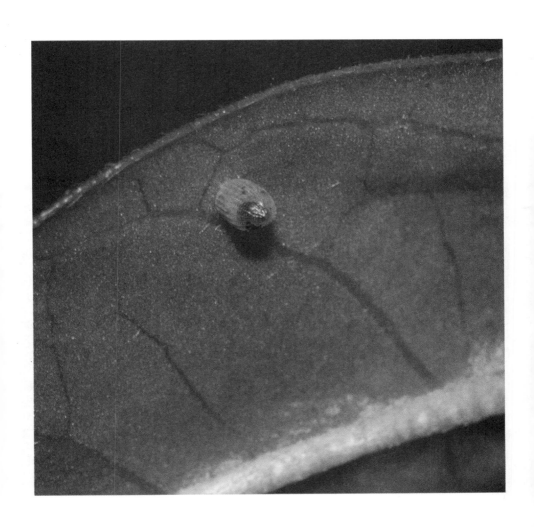

The caterpillar
is very hungry.
She eats her eggshell.
Munch!

She grows bigger.

Leaves are yummy.

Crunch!

Other insects
join the feast.
Red aphids (AY-fids)
slurp sap.

Bees slurp nectar.

Spiders spin webs
to trap meals.

The caterpillar grows
even bigger.

Soon she will be too big
for her own skin!

To keep growing,
she must shed her skin.
This is called *molting*.

Her old skin splits open.
She wiggles out.

She has a new

set of stripes.

She is always hungry.

Her body is
done growing.
She has molted
four times.

She spits up a blob
of sticky stuff.
She sticks to it
and hangs upside down.

The caterpillar molts one last time.
She has formed a sac around herself.

The sac is called a
chrysalis (KRISS-uh-liss).

Many changes are
going on inside.
The caterpillar is
changing into a butterfly!

Now the chrysalis is
almost see-through.

After ten days or so,
the sac opens.

A butterfly pops out!

But she is too weak to fly.

She holds on to the sac.

She pumps fluid

into her new wings.

Her wings dry in the sun.

Now the butterfly flies
and looks for food.

She has not eaten

in two weeks!

The butterfly flies
from flower to flower.

She unrolls her tongue.

It is like a straw.

She sips sweet nectar.

Soon she finds
a winter home
with other butterflies.

It is time to mate.

Our little butterfly
lays her eggs
under the leaf
of a plant.

A few days later,
a caterpillar
eats its way
out of its shell.

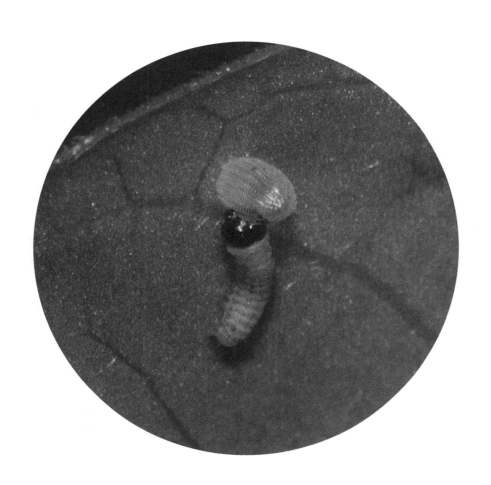

The little caterpillar
is very hungry.

Can you guess what
happens next?